ANN ARBOR DISTRICT LIBRARY
31621210802217

WITHDRAWN

In 1927 **Charles Lindbergh** flew his plane the *Spirit of St. Louis* in the world's first transatlantic crossing. Because it was important to keep the plane as light as possible, his cat, Patsy, had to stay home.

Cleopatra was a queen of ancient Egypt — a cat-loving country in those times. It is thought she modeled her glamorous eye makeup after the faces of her cats.

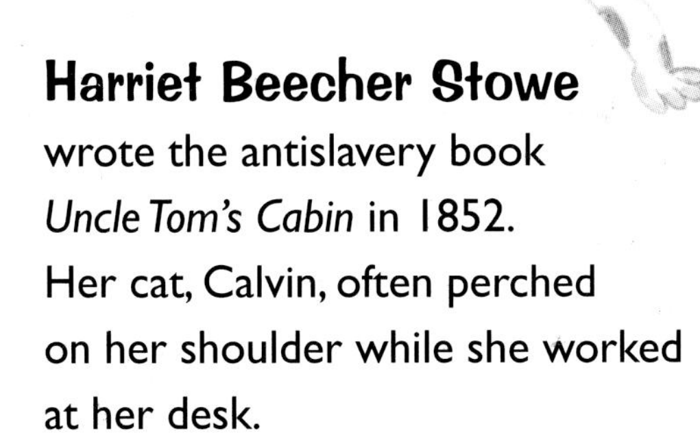

Harriet Beecher Stowe wrote the antislavery book *Uncle Tom's Cabin* in 1852. Her cat, Calvin, often perched on her shoulder while she worked at her desk.

Albert Schweitzer, 1952 Nobel Peace Prize winner, had a cat named Sizi. Sizi sometimes fell asleep on Dr. Schweitzer's arm. Rather than disturb the cat, he would write prescriptions with his other hand.

To Deborah Heiligman,
a purr-fectly gracious friend
— *E.S.*

For Mark, Todd, and Spike
— *G.V.*

Text © 2010 Eileen Spinelli
Illustrations © 2010 Geraldo Valério

All rights reserved

Published in 2010 by Eerdmans Books for Young Readers
an imprint of Wm. B. Eerdmans Publishing Co.
2140 Oak Industrial Dr. NE
Grand Rapids, Michigan 49505
P.O. Box 163, Cambridge CB3 9PU U.K.

www.eerdmans.com/youngreaders

Manufactured at Tien Wah Press in Singapore in April 2010, first printing

10 11 12 13 14 15 16 17 9 8 7 6 5 4 3 2 1

Library of Congress Cataloging-in-Publication Data

Spinelli, Eileen.
Do you have a cat? / by Eileen Spinelli ; illustrated by Geraldo Valério
p. cm.
Summary: Simple, rhyming text introduces historical figures through the cats each owned.
Includes facts about each person.
ISBN 978-0-8028-5351-6 (alk. paper)
[1. Stories in rhyme. 2. Cats — Fiction. 3. Biography — Fiction. 4. History — Fiction.]
I. Valério, Geraldo, 1970- ill. II. Title.
PZ8.3.S759Dn 2010
[E] — dc22
2010001642

The illustrations were rendered in acrylic paint on watercolor paper.
The display type was set in Impress BT.
The text type was set in Gil Sans.

DO YOU HAVE A CAT?

Written by
Eileen Spinelli

Illustrated by
Geraldo Valério

Eerdmans Books for Young Readers

Grand Rapids, Michigan • Cambridge, U.K.

Do you have a cat?

A tabby cat? A Siamese?

A dainty cat? Or one with fleas?

Or maybe one who was a stray

and living in an alleyway?

Do **YOU** have a cat?

St. Martin de Porres had a cat.

Many cats. He took them in —

cats with scratches, cats too thin,

sickly cats too weak to run.

Martin cared for every one.

Do **YOU** have a cat?

Domenico Scarlatti had a cat.
A curious cat. One who explored
the great composer's harpsichord.
She walked the keys, enjoyed the tone,
created music of her own.

Do **YOU** have a cat?

IVANHOE

Sir Walter Scott had a cat.
A tough tomcat — you dogs beware!
This cat would rather fight than share.
He'd race to lunch all hungry-eyed
while clouting Scott's big dogs aside.

Do **YOU** have a cat?

Florence Nightingale had a cat.
A cat so soothing and devoted
that Miss Nightingale once noted
cats made good companions for
people feeling sick or sore.

Do **YOU** have a cat?

Jenny Lind had a cat.
A quiet cat who used to sit
with Jenny while she sang to it.
People smiled who passed along
enchanted by the sight and song.

Do **YOU** have a cat?

MARC

Cleopatra had a cat
(a country full to be precise)
who often chased the palace mice.
This queen considered cats to be
as sacred as her family.

Do **YOU** have a cat?

Calvin Coolidge had a cat.
A gray striped cat who was content
to drape around the president,
and played the part of scarf so well —
cat or scarf? 'Twas hard to tell!

Do **YOU** have a cat?

Henri Matisse had a cat.

A favorite cat as black as coal

who seemed to soothe the painter's soul.

A gentle cat who often kept

the artist cozy while he slept.

Do **YOU** have a cat?

Harriet Beecher Stowe had a cat.
So did **Queen Victoria** — it's true.
Charles Lindbergh,
Albert Schweitzer,
all of them had cats . . .

Do **YOU?**

Do you have a cat?

A playful cat that's lots of fun?

An outdoor cat who likes to run?

A cat who has a favorite chair?

Or one who steals your underwear?

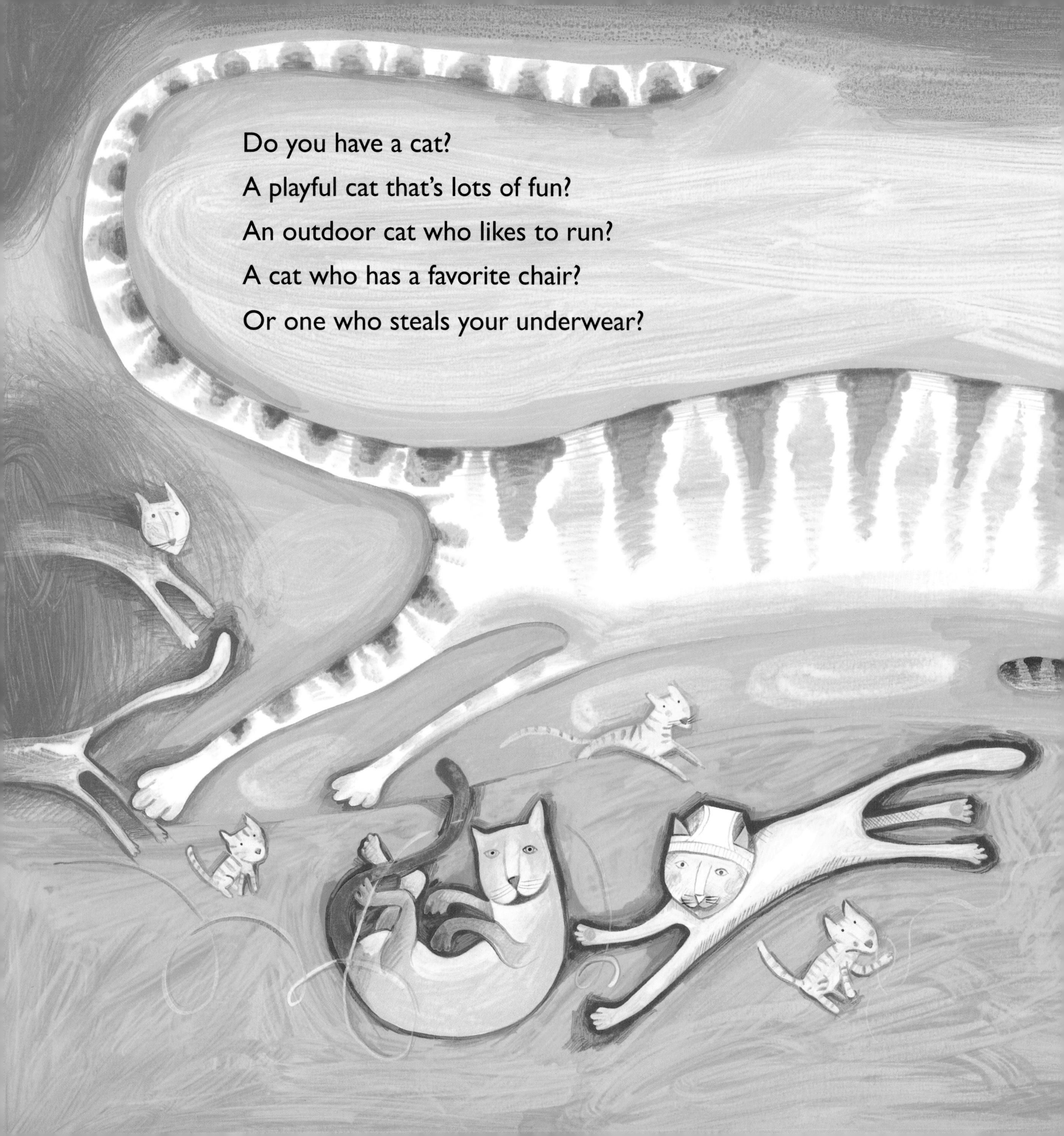

A moody cat? A cat that's brave?
A cat who tends to misbehave?
A cat who likes to caterwaul
is better than no cat at all!

Do **YOU** have a cat?

The Italian composer **Domenico Scarlatti** was born in Naples, Italy, in 1685. It is said that his cat Pulcinella gave him the idea for the sonata called *The Cat's Fugue*.

Florence Nightingale improved the science of nursing in the 1800s and helped make hospitals more sanitary. Her cat Quiz sometime rode the train with her to and from London.

Calvin Coolidge was the 30th president of the United States. Once when his cat Tiger went missing, Mr. Coolidge alerted local radio stations to put out the word. Happily, Tiger was found.

Jenny Lind was one of the best-known singers of the nineteenth century. People called her the "Swedish Nightingale." She became famous after she was overheard singing to her cat.